THE BOXC...

THE MYSTERY OF THE WILD PONIES
THE MYSTERY IN THE COMPUTER GAME
THE HONEYBEE MYSTERY
THE MYSTERY AT THE CROOKED HOUSE
THE HOCKEY MYSTERY
THE MYSTERY OF THE MIDNIGHT DOG
THE MYSTERY OF THE SCREECH OWL
THE SUMMER CAMP MYSTERY
THE COPYCAT MYSTERY
THE HAUNTED CLOCK TOWER MYSTERY
THE MYSTERY OF THE TIGER'S EYE
THE DISAPPEARING STAIRCASE MYSTERY
THE MYSTERY ON BLIZZARD MOUNTAIN
THE MYSTERY OF THE SPIDER'S CLUE
THE CANDY FACTORY MYSTERY
THE MYSTERY OF THE MUMMY'S CURSE
THE MYSTERY OF THE STAR RUBY
THE STUFFED BEAR MYSTERY
THE MYSTERY OF ALLIGATOR SWAMP
THE MYSTERY AT SKELETON POINT
THE TATTLETALE MYSTERY
THE COMIC BOOK MYSTERY
THE GREAT SHARK MYSTERY
THE ICE CREAM MYSTERY
THE MIDNIGHT MYSTERY
THE MYSTERY IN THE FORTUNE COOKIE
THE BLACK WIDOW SPIDER MYSTERY
THE RADIO MYSTERY
THE MYSTERY OF THE RUNAWAY GHOST
THE FINDERS KEEPERS MYSTERY
THE MYSTERY OF THE HAUNTED BOXCAR
THE CLUE IN THE CORN MAZE
THE GHOST OF THE CHATTERING BONES
THE SWORD OF THE SILVER KNIGHT
THE GAME STORE MYSTERY
THE MYSTERY OF THE ORPHAN TRAIN
THE VANISHING PASSENGER
THE GIANT YO-YO MYSTERY
THE CREATURE IN OGOPOGO LAKE
THE ROCK 'N' ROLL MYSTERY
THE SECRET OF THE MASK
THE SEATTLE PUZZLE
THE GHOST IN THE FIRST ROW
THE BOX THAT WATCH FOUND
A HORSE NAMED DRAGON
THE GREAT DETECTIVE RACE
THE GHOST AT THE DRIVE-IN MOVIE

THE MYSTERY OF THE TRAVELING TOMATOES
THE SPY GAME
THE DOG-GONE MYSTERY
THE VAMPIRE MYSTERY
SUPERSTAR WATCH
THE SPY IN THE BLEACHERS
THE AMAZING MYSTERY SHOW
THE PUMPKIN HEAD MYSTERY
THE CUPCAKE CAPER
THE CLUE IN THE RECYCLING BIN
MONKEY TROUBLE
THE ZOMBIE PROJECT
THE GREAT TURKEY HEIST
THE GARDEN THIEF
THE BOARDWALK MYSTERY
THE MYSTERY OF THE FALLEN TREASURE
THE RETURN OF THE GRAVEYARD GHOST
THE MYSTERY OF THE STOLEN SNOWBOARD
THE MYSTERY OF THE WILD WEST BANDIT
THE MYSTERY OF THE SOCCER SNITCH
THE MYSTERY OF THE GRINNING GARGOYLE
THE MYSTERY OF THE MISSING POP IDOL
THE MYSTERY OF THE STOLEN DINOSAUR BONES
THE MYSTERY AT THE CALGARY STAMPEDE
THE SLEEPY HOLLOW MYSTERY
THE LEGEND OF THE IRISH CASTLE
THE CELEBRITY CAT CAPER
HIDDEN IN THE HAUNTED SCHOOL
THE ELECTION DAY DILEMMA
THE DOUGHNUT WHODUNIT
THE ROBOT RANSOM
THE LEGEND OF THE HOWLING WEREWOLF
THE DAY OF THE DEAD MYSTERY
THE HUNDRED-YEAR MYSTERY
THE SEA TURTLE MYSTERY
SECRET ON THE THIRTEENTH FLOOR
THE POWER DOWN MYSTERY
MYSTERY AT CAMP SURVIVAL
THE MYSTERY OF THE FORGOTTEN FAMILY
NEW! THE SKELETON KEY MYSTERY
NEW! SCIENCE FAIR SABOTAGE

THE BOXCAR CHILDREN®

CREATED BY
GERTRUDE CHANDLER WARNER

INTERACTIVE
MYSTERY

TROUBLE ON THE
WILD WEST EXPRESS

ILLUSTRATED BY HOLLIE HIBBERT

ALBERT WHITMAN & COMPANY
CHICAGO, ILLINOIS

TROUBLE ON THE
WILD WEST EXPRESS

INTERACTIVE
MYSTERY

CHOOSE A PATH.
FOLLOW THE CLUES.
SOLVE THE MYSTERY!

Can you help the Boxcar Children crack the case? Follow the directions at the end of each section to decide what the Aldens do next. But beware—some routes will end the story before the case is solved. After you finish one path, go back and follow the other paths to see how it all turns out!

IN THE MINE

Benny Alden peered down the long tunnel. It was dimly lit by the beam from his flashlight. The air was still and dusty. It seemed like the tunnel might go on forever.

"Benny, don't go too far ahead," called Henry, Benny's older brother. Footsteps echoed from behind him, and a moment later, a tour group came around the corner. Among the group were Benny's siblings: Henry, the oldest at fourteen, and Benny's sisters, Jessie and Violet, who were twelve and ten. A guide led the group with a bright lantern.

"Where does that tunnel go?" Benny asked.

The tour guide, a young woman named Alex, held her lantern out so everyone could see where Benny was pointing. The walls were dark-brown

1

and red rock, supported by large wooden beams. In the middle sat a dust-covered, metal mining cart, which was taller than Benny and had four big wheels. The cart was resting on its side, off the tracks that stretched down the floor of the tunnel.

"That reminds me of our boxcar!" Benny said.

"Yes, it does bring back memories," Jessie replied. After their parents had passed away, the four Alden children had lived in an old boxcar in the woods. That was before they'd moved in with their grandfather in Greenfield, Connecticut. Now the boxcar was a playhouse in Grandfather's yard. Mrs. McGregor, the Aldens' housekeeper, kept the boxcar clean and tidy. She even touched up the red paint once a year in the spring—but once, a long time ago, it had been just as dusty as the mining cart in the tunnel.

"That's where the mine railway goes," Alex said. "Back when the mine was being used, the miners would put ore in carts and use the rails to bring it to the surface."

"Did they ever find anything?" Benny asked. He loved looking for hidden treasures. "Like gold?"

Alex shook her head. "Sadly, no. This mine was only used for a few years before they gave up."

"Even though it's called Nugget Mine?" said Violet with a little smile.

Jessie chuckled. "The people who named it that must have been hopeful they would find lots of gold nuggets."

"Maybe too hopeful," Henry added.

"Exactly right," Alex said. "Let's continue on the tour, and I'll tell you more about that." The guide waved the lantern and continued on down the main tunnel.

Benny walked along with his brother and sisters, pausing to look down every dark tunnel. The children had been planning this trip with Grandfather all winter. Jessie had done most of the research, looking up different tours in the western United States. The one they'd chosen, the Wild West Express, included a ride aboard a steam train and stops modeled after the Old West. Now, after planning for so long, Benny could hardly believe they were deep inside a real gold mine.

As they walked, Alex explained more about

the mine. "Even though Henry Wilson, the man who chose to dig here, named the mine after gold nuggets, in truth, he never found any gold here at all. This was common back in the eighteen hundreds. Rumors of gold brought thousands of settlers west, hoping to strike it rich. But in the end, it was very rare to find gold or other valuable minerals, like turquoise and fire opal. This mine and the town where the miners lived was only in operation for a few years before Wilson gave up."

"What would have happened if he'd found gold?" Henry asked.

"During that time, you would make what's called a mining claim," Alex said. "That meant you were claiming the land in order to search for gold or minerals. Then you owned any of the valuables you dug up."

"What happened if someone was already living there?" Jessie asked. "Even if they hadn't made a claim?"

"That happened all the time," Alex said. "The law was set up back then so that if you made a claim through the United States government, then the land and whatever was buried there belonged to you. Anyone else, such as Native Americans who already lived there, had to leave."

"Hmm," Jessie said, pressing her lips together.

A man who had been taking notes in a little notebook cleared his throat. He was wearing a cowboy hat and real cowboy boots. Benny thought he looked like the type of man who had lived back in the days when the mine had been open.

"What happened after the mine closed?" the man asked. "In 1845, if my notes serve?"

"Yes. In 1845, after a few years of work and no luck, the people who were living here and digging in the mine got frustrated and left," Alex said. "Some of them stayed awhile, but in the end, everyone left. For many years, Nugget Mine was a ghost town."

Benny's eyes got big. "A ghost town!" he said. "Haunted?"

Jessie laughed. "No, Benny. That just means no one lived there."

"Oh," Benny said. He was a little disappointed.

The man with the cowboy hat scribbled more notes in his notebook. "I see, I see," he mumbled.

"And what of Nugget Mine now?"

"I read that some people still believe the rumors," Henry said. "They think there really are valuable minerals here and that the miners gave up too soon." He had read the brochure about the mine several times on their long flight from Connecticut to Nevada.

"There are a few rumors," said Alex. "But no real mining has been done in decades. Sometimes people sneak in and poke around. But it's very dangerous to wander around the mines without a guide."

The man with the cowboy hat nodded and continued to take notes. "These days, Nugget Mine is mostly a tourist spot and a place where geologists and historians visit," he said. "The population is just over four hundred."

"Yes. Many of the people who work here also live right here in town," Alex added. "Including Mr. Kinsey, the engineer. He drives the tour train."

Alex came to a stop at two big barriers shaped like X's. She pointed back the way they'd come.

"Anyway, this is as far as the tour goes," she said.

"Let's turn around and head back up to the surface. We have a fun activity planned. Then we'll catch the train for the next part of the tour. But let's hurry. Mr. Kinsey is very strict about leaving on time!"

Benny huffed. He wanted to keep going farther into the mine. But he followed Alex back up the sloped walkway. Then, as the group passed a shadowy tunnel, Benny thought he heard a noise come from the shadows. He pointed his flashlight and saw a shape. But he let out a sigh when he saw it was only the abandoned minecart they had seen earlier.

"What's wrong, Benny?" Violet asked.

Henry and Jessie stopped, too, so they wouldn't get separated.

"I just thought I heard something," Benny said. "I hoped maybe it was a gho—"

All four Aldens froze when another noise echoed from the dark tunnel. It sounded like it could be a voice. Henry pointed his flashlight with Benny's, but the darkness was so thick, they couldn't see past the old cart.

"See?" Benny whispered. "Do you think

someone's down there?"

"I don't know," Henry said. "Alex just said that people sometimes sneak in looking for gold."

"And that it's dangerous," Violet said. "What if someone got hurt down there and needs help?"

Jessie looked over her shoulder. The tour group was heading away, along with the light from Alex's lantern.

"Either way, we should make a decision soon," Jessie said. "What should we do?"

TO GO DEEPER INTO THE MINE, GO TO PAGE 9.

TO HEAD TO THE SURFACE, GO TO PAGE 15.

DEEPER DOWN

"We'll just take a look to make sure everything's okay," Henry said. "But let's make it quick. We don't want to get lost."

Henry led the way down the tunnel, aiming his flashlight in front of him. They passed the old minecart, and Benny turned one of the heavy wheels. It creaked loudly.

The children came to a place lit by a dim bulb. "Anyone down there?" Jessie called, her voice echoing through the dark. "Hello?"

They heard a noise from down the dark tunnel. It sounded like footsteps, as if someone were hurrying away from them.

"Let's go just a little farther," Henry suggested.

"What's that?" Benny asked, pointing.

Another mining cart was up ahead, but unlike the first, this one was upright and sitting on the rails. It took up almost the entire width of the tunnel.

"If we don't move this, we won't be able to get by," Henry said. "We'll have to climb over it."

"Maybe we should go back," Violet said.

"I want to go just a little farther. If someone's down here, they might be lost and need help. We have flashlights and could lead the way out," Henry said.

Henry lifted Benny in first, because he was too short to climb in on his own. He stood at the front of the cart while the others climbed in, one at a time. First Violet, then Jessie, and finally Henry.

"Oof!" Henry's foot bumped against the side of the cart as he clambered in. Metal creaked and groaned, and the cart shuddered. Then Henry felt a breeze on his cheek. They were moving!

"Everyone, hold on!" he cried.

The cart picked up speed as it rolled along the rails, going faster and faster down the dimly lit tunnel. Henry held on to Benny, and Jessie held

Violet as they rocked back and forth, speeding on the rails like they were on a roller coaster at the amusement park. Henry looked around the inside of the cart.

"There has to be a brake somewhere," he said.

"Oh no!" said Violet, pointing her flashlight. "Look!"

Ahead, a mound of fallen rocks blocked the tunnel. If they didn't do something quickly, they were going to crash.

"Found it!" said Henry. He grabbed a lever at the back of the cart and yanked it up. Sparks flew and metal screeched from the wheels on the track. The cart slowed, but it wasn't going to stop in time.

"Get down!" Henry said. They all ducked inside to keep from flying out as the cart ran into the pile of dirt and rock. Henry bumped into Jessie, and Jessie bumped into Violet, who bumped into Benny. Luckily, the brake had slowed them down enough that no one was hurt.

"Oooof," Benny said, brushing himself off. Then he added, "That was fun! Let's do it again!"

Henry chuckled and coughed. "Maybe later."

The four Aldens climbed out of the cart and looked around. The dead end that had stopped the cart looked like it had been caused by a cave-in. Big rocks and a pile of dirt completely blocked the tunnel.

"It's covered in dust," Jessie said, touching it gently with a finger. "It's probably been like this for years."

"I guess there was no one down here after all," Benny said.

"Look at this," Violet said. She knelt down to look at a big rock. It had cracked open when it was struck by the mine cart. Violet pointed her flashlight. Inside, something glittered red and gold.

"Sorry, Violet. We don't have time to look," Jessie said. "It's not safe for us to stay."

"We should head back right away," Henry replied. He gave a big sigh and rubbed a little bruise that was forming on his arm from where he'd bumped into the side of the cart.

The children began walking along the tracks the way they had come.

"I didn't know we'd gone so far," said Jessie,

stopping to take a breather.

"We're deep in the mine," said Henry. "I don't think we are going to make it back before the train leaves."

Violet sighed. "I guess our trip on the Wild West Express is over."

"At least we got a wild ride!" said Benny.

THE END

TO FOLLOW A DIFFERENT PATH, GO TO PAGE 8.

TO THE TOP

"It's too dangerous," Henry said. "We'll tell Alex what we heard and head back to the surface with the rest of the group."

Jessie nodded. "We wouldn't want to miss the train to the next part of the tour," she said.

The four children hurried after the tour group. By the time they caught up, they were almost at the surface. The daylight was very bright compared to the darkness of the tunnels. Benny squinted as his eyes adjusted.

The group walked along a dirt trail, away from the rocky hill where the mine entrance stood. The sky was blue and streaked with clouds. The land around them was light brown and red. Clusters of silver and green sagebrush and desert grass rustled in the breeze. It was nice to have a breath of fresh air again after being in the tunnels.

While they walked, Henry told Alex what the children had heard in the tunnel.

Alex sighed. "Thanks for letting me know," she said. "It's probably nothing. Rocks and gravel get knocked loose every once in a while. It can echo and sound much bigger than it is. But sometimes people sneak in looking for precious gems and gold nuggets. I'll let my manager know. They'll send someone to check it out."

Before long, the group reached a cluster of three buildings. The buildings all had big signs drawn in old-fashioned lettering. Violet read the signs aloud with Benny, who was just learning to read. The signs said *Nugget Mine Visitor Center*, *Education Building*, and *General Offices*.

"Why don't you all rest a minute while I go get ready for our activity," Alex said when they arrived in front of the visitor center. "I'll meet you behind in the backyard in about five minutes."

Behind the visitor center, there was a small yard with several large tubs set out. The tubs were full of dirt the same color as the dirt inside the mine—reddish yellow. Resting along the side of the visitor center in the shade were tall digging shovels and a stack of metal pails.

"I hope the activity involves food," Benny said. "Talking about nuggets so much is making me hungry."

"I don't think you'd want to eat a gold nugget, Benny," Jessie teased.

"You might bite a gold coin to find out if it was real or not," said the man in the group with the notebook. He offered his hand. "My name is Frederick, by the way. My pen name is F. R. Wayne, but you can call me Fred."

The Aldens shook the man's hand one at a time.

"Pen name?" Violet asked. "Are you a writer?"

"Indeed I am," Fred said. "I thought going on this tour would give me the perfect experience to improve my story."

"I want to bite some gold," Benny said.

"Maybe you'll get a chance, Benny," Henry said. He nodded at the tubs of dirt and the shovels. "It looks like our activity might have to do with digging for gold."

Alex came out of the visitor center wearing overalls and gloves. "You're right!" she said. "Everyone, I want you to team up in groups of two. Each team, grab a shovel and a pail."

"I want to be on a team with Jessie today," Benny said. "I can't wait to dig for buried treasure! Will there be a treasure map?"

"I don't think so," Jessie said. "The settlers back in the olden days didn't have maps. They just dug wherever they thought they might find gold!"

"I want to be on a team with Henry," Violet said. "Let's get our shovels."

Once everyone in the tour group had a partner, a shovel, and a pail, they waited for Alex to explain how the activity would work. Alex stood with her own shovel in front of one of the tubs of dirt.

"During the years when the mine was active, miners would bring dirt out on those mining carts to the surface, just like these tubs. They would look through the dirt and use a tool called a 'sluice box' to pan for gold," Alex explained. "Today, you are going to get the chance to do the same thing. This is real dirt that came from in and around the mine."

Alex turned so the group could see another station on the side of the yard near the visitor center. A garden hose was hooked up next to some more tubs full of water. There were also some metal boxes stacked on a table.

"I'll show you how the sluice boxes work one at a time when we get to that part," Alex continued. "But for the first part, each team should fill their pail with dirt. Then, one at a time, you can bring the pails over to the water station. The fun part is that if you find anything, it's yours to keep! It's all included in the ticket you bought as part of the Wild West Express tour."

It was fun but hard work to fill the pail with dirt. Henry did most of the digging, although Violet told him where she wanted him to dig. The dirt was a lot heavier than it looked! By the time they had filled their pail, it was so heavy, Violet had to use both hands to carry it over to Alex at the water station. They were joined by Jessie and Benny, who had their own pail.

"All right, ready to see how the sluice box works?" Alex asked. The children nodded.

Alex showed them the metal box. It was about the size of a folded-up stepladder and had a wire mesh bottom that reminded Benny of a cheese grater.

"Many times back during the Gold Rush times, miners would use these boxes to pan for gold in a river," Alex said. "It works by catching the big rocks, while the rest of the soil gets washed through the grate by running water. We can use it here with these tubs of water and the hose."

Alex set the sluice box on top of one of the water tubs and handed Benny a garden spade. Benny carefully chose some dirt he thought might have treasure inside. He scooped from his pail into the box.

Next, Alex held the garden hose over the box. As the water ran over the dirt and rock, the soil seemed to melt through the grate. After a few moments, only a few bigger rocks were left. One of them glimmered silver.

"What's that?" said Benny. He picked up the rock to look more closely. Stuck to the stone was a soda-can tab, which he picked off.

Alex chuckled. "Looks like you just had a real gold-digging experience," she said. "Most people who mined for gold didn't find any. I'm sorry you only found garbage."

But Benny wasn't disappointed at all. He washed off the soda-can tab and held it up in the sunlight. He had found it all on his own. "It'll be my lucky garbage!" he said.

Next it was Violet and Henry's turn. After Alex washed the soil into the tub with the hose water, there weren't any rocks left in the sluice tray. Henry squeezed Violet's shoulder when she gave a tiny sigh of disappointment.

After the groups had all taken their turns at the sluice station, a honk came from the parking lot. Alex turned off the water spigot and set down the hose.

"That's the tour bus," she called, waving everyone over. "I had a great time showing y'all the mine today."

Some of the people from the tour had found stones during the dig: white quartz and brown agate. One woman even found a rock with fool's gold in it. It looked just like gold, but Alex explained that it was a different mineral called iron pyrite.

"It looked just as neat," Violet said. "I sure wish I'd found something."

"We'll have better luck next time," Henry said.

"Yeah, Violet! Let's head to the bus and get a good seat," Benny said, grabbing Violet's hand. "I can't wait to tell Grandfather about the mine and the dirt and the sluice box and the lucky charm I found!"

Jessie laughed as she joined them. "I'm sure he'll be just as excited to hear about it," she said.

The Aldens followed the rest of the group out to the parking lot where the shuttle bus was parked. It would be a short ride back to town, where they would catch the train to continue their tour.

"You didn't find anything either?" Fred asked when he saw them. He gave a heavy sigh. "I really wanted to find something. Striking gold would have been such an exciting way to jump-start my imagination and get me out of this writer's block!"

"It's the authentic gold-digging experience,"

Benny said, repeating what Alex had said.

The children lined up to board the bus. But right before they got on, Violet paused. Something had caught her eye.

CONTINUE TO PAGE 24

ON THE TRAIN AGAIN

"Wait a second," said Violet. She scampered out into the desert beyond the parking lot. A red rock had caught the light just right, glittering with brilliant peach and red streaks. She ran back to the shuttle bus and jumped on right before the driver closed the door.

"What did you pick up?" Benny asked when she sat with the rest of them.

Fred, who was sitting across the aisle of the bus, leaned over. His eyes widened when he saw the glittering rock Violet had found. "That looks like it might be fire opal. Look how it shines! It could mean there are precious gems here after all. You know, you could submit a mining claim, just like the settlers of the Old West!"

"Should I tell Alex?" Violet asked.

"This is outside of the tour area. So that means it's free range!" Frank said. "Finders keepers."

Violet looked to Jessie and Henry, who shrugged.

"It would make a nice addition to your rock collection," Jessie said. "It's very pretty."

Violet nodded and put the rock in her bag. She still felt uneasy about keeping it. But the shuttle was already on its way back to town. If she decided to change her mind, she would have to do it later.

The shuttle ride to town was only a few minutes. The road was bumpy and unpaved. Jessie looked out the window. Small houses popped up along the road, and then suddenly they were in the small town of Nugget Mine, named for the very mine they had just visited.

The shuttle stopped at the station, where the train was waiting on the rails. The train cars were pulled by a black steam locomotive with red wheels, decorated with a banner that read *Wild West Express: Four-Day Tour* on the side.

"All aboard!" the conductor shouted on the crowded platform. "Anyone with valuables may place them in the safe at the rear of the sleeping cars. This includes any souvenirs you may have found out at the mine. All aboard!"

"Excuse me," Alex said to the conductor over the noise on the platform. "These children heard a sound down in the mine. They think there might have been someone else down there."

"Oh dear," said the conductor. "I will let the station authorities know. Now, all passengers should go aboard the train. And, Alex, I believe you're running late for your stage call."

Alex gasped. "Oh no, you're right! I have to go. I'll see you all in a little bit."

"Stage call?" Henry asked, but Alex was already hurrying away.

"All aboard!" the conductor called again.

As the children approached the train, they passed Mr. Kinsey, the engineer. He was a tall man with spectacles perched on his nose. He kept checking his watch and barely noticed the Aldens as they passed.

"We'll be late at this rate," he said gruffly to himself.

"Do we have any valuables we need to keep in the safe?" Jessie asked her siblings. "I'm going to keep my laptop with me. I want to write about everything we saw and did today."

"I just have my pop-top," Benny said. "But Violet should put her shiny red rock in the safe. It could be valuable!"

Benny spoke loudly. Some of the other people on the platform were interested in what he was talking about. One of those people was Mr. Kinsey.

"Valuable?" he asked. "Did you find something back at the mine?"

"Yes!" said Benny. He held his pop-top up so that Mr. Kinsey could see it. Then, when the engineer did not respond, Benny motioned to Violet and her red rock. "Do you know how to submit a mining claim? Maybe Violet could do that, just like in the old days!"

Mr. Kinsey let out a loud huff of air through his nose, nearly blowing his spectacles off his face. "Hmph!" he said. "You're just like every other tourist who comes through here." And with that, he briskly walked away, heading to the front of the

train where the driver's compartment was.

"That seemed a little rude," Henry said with a frown.

"Benny, I don't want to submit a mining claim," Violet said. "I would be happy just to add the rock to my collection."

"Okay," Benny said. "But if you change your mind, I want to be the first to know."

After the children were on board, there was a lurch beneath their feet. The train was moving. At a slow and steady pace, they headed to the next stop on their tour.

The Aldens found Grandfather in the dining car. He was just ordering lunch.

"Oh, children!" he said. "Did you have fun at the mine? Here, pick out something to eat. I'm sure you're hungry."

During their meal in the dining car, Violet and Benny told Grandfather about everything they had seen and done that day in Nugget Mine. Grandfather listened with a smile.

"Sounds like you had a great time," he said. "I went to the town museum while you were all out at the mine. I also passed some costumed folks on horseback. I wonder what they're up to."

Just then, they all heard whooping and hollering through the open train windows. All four children and Grandfather hurried to see what was going on.

Outside, five people on horseback galloped alongside the train. They wore costume vests and hats, with bright bandannas pulled up over their mouths to hide their faces.

"Bandits!" Benny yelped with delight.

"This here's a train robbery," the leader of the bandits shouted with a broad flourish of his hat. "And we're robbin' your safe!"

"Oh no, whatever shall we do?" said a voice over the train speaker. It was Mr. Kinsey from the driver's compartment. He didn't sound very enthusiastic. "Please, not the safe. Have mercy."

"Them's the breaks in the Wild West! Yeehaw!" cried the bandit.

The bandits got closer on their horses until they could reach the ladders bolted near the doors of the train. They clambered aboard, hooting and hollering. When they entered the dining car, one of the bandits approached the Aldens.

"What have we got here?" the bandit asked in a familiar voice. She leaned close and winked. The Aldens gasped. It was Alex!

"Turn out your pockets, little boy!" she said to Benny.

"I've only got this," Benny said, holding out the soda-can tab. "Please don't take it!" He giggled.

"Well, there's a mighty fine trinket," said Alex the bandit. She smirked at Grandfather and the other Aldens. "But I don't want no trouble from this lot. I guess it's your lucky day, little man." Then she followed the rest of the whooping bandits through the dining car, toward the front of the train to entertain more of the passengers.

After the bandits had moved on, Jessie noticed something out the opposite window and went to look. Henry joined her.

"What's up?" he asked.

"I thought I saw someone..." said Jessie. "Look!"

Along the side of the train, a rider in a cowboy hat galloped their horse alongside the train. A bandanna covered most of their face. Now that the bandit actors were on board, the train was picking up speed, but that didn't stop this rider.

"Is that one of the reenactment people?" Henry asked.

"I don't think so," Jessie said.

As the rider approached the rear car, they leaped up to stand on the saddle with impressive balance. Then they jumped from the saddle and grabbed hold of the ladder on the side of the train car, slipping into the train. After its rider was gone, the horse disappeared around the back of the train.

Jessie and Henry looked away as the bandit actors gave a little bow at the front of the dining car. The tour group applauded and cheered, especially for Alex, who took off her hat and waved it over her head.

The bandit reenactment was done. But if all of the actors were in the dining car, who was the rider at the back of the train?

CONTINUE TO PAGE 33

WELCOME TO THE WILD WEST

The Aldens slept in a sleeper car they shared with Grandfather. It was surprisingly comfortable to sleep on the train, even in the narrow bunk beds. In many ways, it reminded Jessie of when they had lived in the boxcar.

Early the next morning, they awoke to the train whistle. Outside the window, they could see the wide, golden Nevada landscape spread under a blue sky.

Henry stretched. "Wow, we're already at the next stop," he said.

"What's the next stop?" Benny asked, sitting up.

Violet took out the tour pamphlet. "It says here, after Nugget Mine and an encounter with bandits, we'll stop at Regions Station, where we can have a living history tour of a western settlement."

"Living history?" Benny asked.

"That's when actors perform like they're living in a different time period," Jessie said. "It's sort of like walking on the set of a movie."

"Look, they even have an old-fashioned saloon!" Henry said, looking out the window.

"I hope it's not too old-fashioned," Grandfather said as he combed his hair. "Back in the eighteenth and nineteenth centuries, children and women weren't allowed in saloons, you know."

"I hope not too," Benny said. "I could really use some breakfast."

A small group of performers waited eagerly on the platform as the train arrived. They were all dressed in Old West clothing, the women wearing long dresses and hats and the men in long coats and neckties. They greeted the tour group cheerfully as everyone disembarked.

"Welcome to Region Springs, y'all!" said one man. He wore a stovepipe hat, and his bushy, black mustache shook as he spoke with a thick southern accent. "I'm Mayor Clements. If there's anything you need, you let me know, ya hear?"

"I hear ya!" Benny exclaimed with a big grin.

It was a cool, sunny morning. The train platform was much smaller than back at Nugget Mine, simple and made of wood with a small set of stairs that led to the main street of the town. The town had one street with two rows of buildings, all built of brick and timber and decorated with signs in old-timey lettering. In the distance, an old-fashioned water tower was just visible, lit by the morning sun.

"Did you sleep well?" asked a voice from over their shoulder. Alex had changed out of her bandit costume and was wearing an old-fashioned blouse and skirt. She smiled.

"Good morning, Alex!" Violet said. "You were great yesterday."

"Thanks! I'm glad you think so. There was a bit of a problem in the beginning, but I'm glad it didn't ruin the show."

"Problem?" Henry asked.

"Yes. One of our performance horses went missing," Alex said. "But I'm sure by now he's turned up. How did y'all sleep last night on the train?"

"We slept great," Benny said. "But now we're hungry. Where's the saloon?"

"Right across the street," Alex said. "I'm ready for some grits too."

"Grits?" Benny asked.

"That's what we eat for breakfast out here in the Wild West," Alex said. "Don't worry. It's like oatmeal."

"Would you eat with us?" Violet asked.

"Of course!"

The saloon looked like an old-fashioned saloon on the outside, with double swinging doors and hitching posts and a water trough for horses. But inside, it looked more like a restaurant with tables and booths. The air smelled like eggs and pancakes. The Aldens got a table with Grandfather and Alex, and together they ordered breakfast from the friendly waiter.

While the children ate, they recognized other tour group members arriving for breakfast, including Mr. Kinsey, the engineer, and Fred, the author with the notebook. While Fred drank a mug of coffee and chatted loudly with another tour guest, Mr. Kinsey sat at a table in the corner by himself, reading a thick book. He kept checking his watch with a frown on his face and a wrinkle in his forehead.

"Mr. Kinsey seems grumpy," Henry said. "Is he all right?"

"He's always like this," Alex said. "I think he'd prefer to read those big books of his rather than drive the train for the tour groups, but I guess being an expert on American history doesn't pay the bills."

Clank! Everyone jumped as Fred pounded his fist on the table, rattling his dishes and silverware. Even his breakfast guest stood up in surprise.

"This isn't what I paid for!" Fred exclaimed, leaning toward the other man. "I wanted a real experience, not a group of costumed bandits putting on a show for children. At this rate, I'll never be inspired out of my writer's block. If something interesting doesn't happen soon, I might have to create some *real* drama myself!"

The small salon went silent, and everyone looked at Fred. He cleared his throat before laughing nervously. People went back to their conversations,

except for Mr. Kinsey, who glared at Fred from across the room. Fred didn't notice.

"Speaking of the bandits and the excitement, that reminds me," Henry said. "Jessie, why don't you ask Alex about what we saw yesterday."

"Yesterday?" Alex asked.

Jessie nodded. "When the bandits were robbing the train, we saw another rider with their horse on the tracks. It looked like they were in the rear car. They jumped from their horse right onto the train. Was that part of the show?"

Alex tilted her head and furrowed her brow. "No...it should have just been the five of us. Usually, there are six, but as I said, one of the horses must have wandered off at the last minute."

"Maybe they found the horse and the rider came and caught up," said Henry.

Alex gave a small smile and nodded. "That's probably it," she said. Still, she didn't seem sure.

"Isn't the rear car where the safe is?" Violet asked. She touched her bag where she was keeping the red fire opal she'd found. It was still there, safe and hidden.

"Yes, the conductor usually keeps the safe there," said Alex. "Though no one really uses it for valuables like jewelry anymore. Most people just keep the rocks they get at Nugget Mine there, since they're big and bulky."

"And I asked the attendant to keep my slippers in there, just so he had something to do," Grandfather said.

"Well, without more information, there's not a lot we can do," said Jessie. "Let's finish breakfast and get ready for the next part of the tour. Alex, what's on the schedule for today?"

Alex brightened with a big smile. "Oh, there's tons to do here in Region Station. So much that you really can't do it all in one day. Two of my favorites are the Pony Express demonstration and the nature tour out to the water tower, though I might be a little biased. I'm the guide on that one."

"I want to see the horses!" Violet said. Then she turned to Alex. "Sorry. I just love seeing horses up close."

Alex gave a big smile. "No need to apologize. It's your decision!"

Trouble on the Wild West Express

"We might be able to see some wild animals out on the desert tour," Henry said. "Like a Gila monster or a mountain lion! Hmm...both are really good options."

"I'll go to whichever one you don't," Grandfather said. "That way we can share stories after. Now, children...which do you want to try?"

IF THE CHILDREN GO ON A DESERT TOUR, GO TO PAGE 42.

IF THE CHILDREN TRY OUT THE PONY EXPRESS, GO TO PAGE 51.

DESERT RIDE

"We've spent enough time in town," said Jessie. "My vote is for the desert tour."

"Great choice," said Alex. "Besides all the wild critters, there are cacti and wildflowers. And some cool rocks too."

At this, Violet perked up. "I'll bring my camera," she said.

"Maybe we'll find more treasure!" added Benny.

"Sounds like we'd all like to go," Henry laughed. "What do you think, Grandfather?"

"Works for me," said Grandfather. "I will visit the ponies at the stable, then. Be sure to take lots of pictures, and I'll do the same!"

The Aldens finished their breakfast. Outside the saloon, a horse-drawn wagon rumbled by, and a man in a round cap stood next to a water barrel doing card tricks. Two cowboys on horseback chatted in drawling accents. They tipped their wide-brimmed hats to the Aldens.

"Howdy," said one of the cowboys.

"Howdy!" Benny called back. "Boy, I'm gonna need a hat."

They waved so long to Grandfather and went with Alex to wait near the train station. There, a sign read *Desert Adventure Pickup*.

"The tour will be on a truck," Alex explained. "There it is now!"

A big truck rumbled up the road. It was pulling a flatbed trailer with bench seats built in so passengers could ride in the open air. The truck stopped in front of the sign, and the tour group climbed aboard.

"Just like a hayride!" Violet said.

"More like a cactus ride!" Benny said. Then he thought about the prickles on a cactus. "On second thought, maybe just a hayride."

Fred, the author, was also going on the tour. He looked just as excited as he had been in the saloon.

Maybe even more so. He sat next to Benny and took out his binoculars.

"I heard you mention treasure on this tour, back in the saloon," he said. "I hope you're right. Yesterday was all right, but I need something to get out of my writer's block. I need a surprise! Maybe a bear!"

Benny thought about this. "But if we see a bear now, it wouldn't be a surprise anymore," he said.

The man looked confused. He shook his head. "Well, if something exciting doesn't happen, I'll just have to make it happen myself!"

"I doubt we'll see a bear in this part of Nevada, but we might see other animals," Alex said. She spoke up as the driver started the truck, using her loud tour-guide voice. "All right, everyone, hold on! This can be a little bumpy."

It was more than a little bumpy. There was no paved road between the town and the water tower. The truck bounced and rumbled over loose gravel, sending up big clouds of dust behind them. It was a cool morning, and the sky seemed bigger than before. In the distance, Violet saw mountains.

"Rainfall out here in the Nevada desert is only around seven inches a year," Alex said as they traveled. "So of course, back in the eighteen hundreds, having a water tower was very important. Today, we mostly use it for mining demonstrations and to service the train. The locomotive is a steam engine, so it requires water to run."

"Violet, look," Benny said, pointing. "Out there!"

A ways off, to the left of the truck, six orange creatures grazed on sagebrush and grass. They looked like small deer, with curved antlers and black-and-white markings on their faces.

"Pronghorn," Alex said, noticing the animals. "They're often called American antelope, but they aren't related to antelope at all. They're actually more closely related to giraffes."

"What else lives out here?" Violet asked.

"Pronghorn are pretty common. Other animals you might see include foxes and wolves, bats, tortoises, and many types of birds," Alex said.

"And snakes!" said Fred.

"Yes, Nevada is famous for our snakes," said Alex. "Which reminds me. When we're out at the water tower, don't go poking around in the brush or anywhere off the path where it's warm and sunny. Some of the snakes out here are dangerous. We don't want to see anyone getting bit."

"I'm not afraid of snakes," Fred said. "The more dangerous, the more exciting. And the more exciting, the better!"

The group enjoyed the rest of the ride watching the scenery. Violet took photos of white and yellow wildflowers growing among sagebrush, and an eagle as it called from above.

"Is this really a desert?" Benny asked. "I always thought the desert was a lot of sand and no plants or animals."

Alex smiled. "Deserts all over the world are full of life. Plants and animals always have a way surviving. It just might look different here than in a forest or a field."

Violet took in a big breath of fresh air. "It's beautiful," she said.

The truck pulled up in the shadow of the water tower. The area around the tower was mostly cleared of sagebrush. The water tower itself was a big, round thing made of wood, with a cone for a roof. A long chute jutted out of the bottom and led to a zigzagging trough.

"Here's the trough we use for the mining demonstrations," Alex said. "And these pans are the same ones prospectors used all those years ago. But as I mentioned, today the water is reserved for servicing our train. Steam locomotives require a lot of water to travel."

Violet and Benny picked up the dusty old pans. It felt as if they had stepped into the past.

The author, Fred, was not impressed. "Hmph. That little girl found a fire opal back at Nugget Mine, but the only rocks I've found are the ones in my shoes!" He wandered away, looking around the trough and the area near the bottom of the water tower.

Alex went on to tell them more about the water tower, pointing up at it as she did. "This water tower was built in 1869, the same year the Central Pacific Railroad was connected to the Union Pacific Railroad in Utah. When those two railroads were connected, they formed the First Transcontinental

Railroad. Most water towers don't last longer than a few decades, but this one has been maintained for historical purposes—"

Alex stopped short when Fred let out a frightened shout from the other side of the water tower, where he'd been poking around.

"Snake!" he yelled.

A rattling noise came from the brush near where Fred was standing. It sounded like the maracas Benny had played with during band class. As Fred backed away, they could see a big brown snake coiled in a stack of rocks where Fred had been poking about.

"Rattlesnake!" Fred said again.

"Everyone, stay calm," Alex said. "If you leave it alone, it will leave you—"

Before anyone could stop him, Fred grabbed one of the pickaxes from the base of the water tower and yanked it upward. But at the top of Fred's swing, the sharp point of the pick sank right into the side of the wooden water tower.

"Uh-oh," Alex said. "Everyone, get back!"

The water tower creaked. Then it groaned.

Then, the pickax popped out and water started to pour from the hole.

"Is there any way to plug it?" Henry asked.

But he was too late. As the water came out, the wood panels on the side of the tower splintered and broke. A big hole burst open. Gallons and gallons of water gushed out. Some of it poured into the trough, but most of it splashed to the ground, causing a muddy mess.

In just a minute, it was over. The last drops of water trickled out.

"Well, that's that," Alex said with a big sigh. "Without the water to fill the steam engine, we won't be able to continue. Sorry, everyone. The rest of the Wild West Express tour will have to be canceled."

THE END

TO FOLLOW A DIFFERENT PATH, GO TO PAGE 41.

THE PONY EXPRESS

"Let's go see the horses," Benny said. "What's the Pony Express?"

"I bet we'll learn all about it when we go to the demonstration," Jessie assured him. The children finished their breakfast and said so long to Grandfather and Alex outside the saloon.

"I'm taking the group out to the water tower, but you'll have a fun time with Sofia," Alex said. "She's the star of the Pony Express demonstration. She's very talented."

The children followed the signs to the Pony Express stable. It was a bigger building at the end of Main Street. They knew they had reached the right place because of the hay that was scattered everywhere and, of course, because there were four brown horses standing outside the front doors. A small group of people were waiting with them.

"Hello!" called a cheerful voice. Out of the stable came a young woman with dark hair in a braid. She wore a vest, denim jeans, and leather chaps.

"I'm Sofia Vasquez," said the woman. "Welcome to the Wild West Express Pony Express demonstration. I hope y'all are having a great trip so far."

"We sure are," Benny said. "We just came from Nugget Mine yesterday, and I found treasure there!" He showed her his pop-top, which he'd been keeping safe in his pocket.

"Oh yeah? I live in Nugget Mine," Sofia said with a bright smile. "Nice, shiny treasure you found there." She winked.

"Yeah! And my sister Violet found a really pretty red rock. She could submit a mining claim and—" Benny covered his mouth at the end. He had forgotten that Violet didn't want to talk about what she'd found.

Sofia's arched an eyebrow. "Submit a mining claim, eh?" she asked.

"No, no, it's nothing," Violet said. "We're just

glad now to have the chance to see the horses."

Sofia nodded slowly. Then she turned to the rest of the tour group and flashed another big smile.

"We'll go in and see the horses in just a moment. Before we start, I want to tell you a little bit about horse safety," she began.

Violet and her siblings listened carefully while Sofia explained how to behave safely around horses. They learned not to approach horses from the rear and not to pet any horses unless Sofia said it was all right.

"And please, don't feed the horses," Sofia said at the end. "All our horses participate in the yearly Pony Express reenactment. It takes hard work and athletic training, so they're all fed a special diet."

"Just like an Olympic athlete," Benny whispered.

"Just like it," said Sofia. She waved with a friendly gesture. "All right, come on back!"

The children and the rest of the group followed Sofia through the stable. In addition to the horses out front, there were several more horses in the stables. Sofia showed Benny how to use a coat brush on one of the horse's necks, making it look smooth and glossy.

As the children watched, Jessie couldn't get over the idea that she knew Sofia from someplace. "Does she look familiar to you?" Jessie asked Violet.

"Maybe," said Violet, tilting her head. She giggled. "Or maybe we've just seen too many of Grandfather's old westerns."

When the grooming was done, Sofia showed the group the other things that went into caring for horses. Every day, the stables had to be cleaned with a pitchfork and broom. Henry and Jessie took turns cleaning one of the empty stables. By the time they were done, they were both sweating.

"Lastly, my Express riders and I have a little show for you out back," Sofia said as they reached the far end of the stable. There, the barn doors opened into a fenced-in pasture where two mounted riders waited. They were in costume, with tan jackets and bandannas. A third horse was waiting for Sofia near the stable door.

"People used the Pony Express to carry letters from the east all the way to California," Sofia said. "Riders would ride about a hundred miles a day on

horseback and exchange the mail with a new rider at the end of the route. That rider would take the mail and keep going."

"Oh, like a relay race," Henry said. He had run a few relay races as part of track and field for school.

"Yes, exactly," said Sofia. "It was very tiring on both the horses and the riders. Today, we're going to do a miniature version of that. But just a moment—I forgot something important."

Sofia went back into the stable. While they had a minute, Benny tapped Violet's arm.

"Sorry about what I said earlier," Benny said. "I forgot you didn't want to tell people about the rock you found."

"It's okay, Benny," Violet reassured him. "I'm still not sure what I want to do with my stone. I don't want people to think that I'm trying to cause any trouble."

"I understand," Benny said.

"All right, now we can begin!" declared Sofia.

She had come back wearing a handsome cowboy hat, which she'd left inside. With the balance and grace of a cat, Sofia took a running leap and landed lightly on the saddle of her waiting horse.

Sofia put two fingers in her mouth and whistled. The two others rode their horses out into the pasture, far enough away that they looked like little toy cowboys on horseback. Sofia held up an envelope so everyone could see it before slipping it into the pocket of her saddlebag.

"Pony Express riders used special saddlebags to carry the mail. The saddlebags were called 'mochila.' It made it easy to transfer the mail from one rider to the next. When I get to the next rider in this relay race, we'll switch the mochila...Well, you'll see how it works. Just watch!"

Sofia clucked her tongue at her horse and snapped her reins. The horse burst into a gallop, running with incredible speed. When they neared the next rider, Sofia hopped out of the saddle with an impressive flip. The other rider was waiting. He grabbed the mochila off the saddle of Sofia's horse and threw it on his. Then, in a flash, he leaped into the saddle and raced on to the next rider.

"Can you imagine riding a relay like that for a hundred miles?" Jessie asked. "I feel sore just thinking about being in the saddle that long."

"Sofia!" A man's voice came from inside the stable. It was Mr. Kinsey, the engineer from the train, waving his hat in alarm. Sofia rode her horse over when she heard him.

"What's wrong?" she asked.

"You didn't notice? The horses have escaped and are getting into trouble all over town!" Mr. Kinsey said with a huff.

"How did they get out?" asked Jessie. She was sure the stable doors had been locked when they'd come outside.

"Someone must have let them out," said Henry.

Sofia sighed. "Well, I guess that's the end of the demonstration," she said.

The other rider rode up and placed the mochila back on Sofia's horse. Sofia turned back to the tour group. "I'm going to go round up the horses. Since you have some extra time now, I'd suggest you check out the candy shop on Main Street."

"Rounding up the horses is going to be a lot of work," Henry said. "Are you sure you don't want help?"

"I couldn't ask you to do that," Sofia said. "I should have been more careful about keeping the stables closed, so this is something I should take care of. You deserve to enjoy your tour, and the candy shop is really fun. I promise!"

Henry glanced back at his siblings. "What do you think we should do?" he asked.

IF THE ALDENS HELP ROUND UP THE HORSES, GO TO PAGE 60.

IF THE ALDENS GO TO THE CANDY SHOP, GO TO PAGE 68.

ROUNDUP

"Don't worry, Sofia," said Jessie. "We'll help you."

"Are you sure?" Sofia asked. "I can probably take care of it just fine on my own—"

"*We* insist," Henry said with a big smile. "No one should have to round up a whole stable of horses on their own, and you've been kind enough to give us a great demonstration."

Sofia sighed. She seemed a little hesitant to let the children help her, but she nodded in the end.

"Okay," she said. "In that case, it'll be easier if you're on horseback. There are two horses tied out front. Have any of you ridden before?"

"Yes," Jessie said. "All four of us have had lessons. But it will be safest if Benny and Violet ride double with us."

"Benny, you're with me," Henry said. He waved to his brother and sisters. "Come on, let's go."

The horses that had been tied to the hitch at the front of the stable were still there, munching on oats from the feed bags. Henry and Jessie helped Benny and Violet up into the saddles first before climbing up themselves. In a moment, they were ready.

"There were twelve horses in the stable," Sofia said. "The good news is, they should all be wearing bridles, so we won't have worry about using a lasso. We should focus on getting them off the track, so the train can leave on time. As you probably know, Mr. Kinsey is very strict about the schedule...I can round up the rest later if I need to. The most important thing is making sure the tour isn't canceled because of my mistake."

"Got it!" Henry said. "Ready, Benny?"

"Ready!" Benny cheered.

"Hold on tight!"

The Aldens trotted down Main Street a little ways before Henry and Benny split off to look around the train tracks. Right away, they saw two horses grazing just outside of town. When they saw

Henry and Benny approaching, the horses trotted away, swishing their tails playfully.

"All right, Benny," Henry said. "I'm going to try and grab the bridles. When I do, you tie the reins to the saddle horns, all right? Once we have the reins, I think the horses will follow."

The escaped horses weren't afraid of Henry and Benny and didn't gallop away. But they did seem to know they were being naughty. It took a few minutes to get close enough for Henry to reach the reins on the nearest horse.

"Got it!"

Once he had the bridle, the horse followed along just fine. It seemed to know it was time to return to the stable. Henry handed Benny the reins, and Benny wrapped them around the saddle horn. Next, they tracked down the second horse. It took as long as the first had, but it was fun to ride up high on a horse. Benny felt like a real, old-fashioned cowboy.

"All right, that's two of them," Henry said. "Let's bring them back to the stable and find the rest!"

Meanwhile, Jessie and Violet continued trotting

their horse down Main Street. The horses seemed to have calmed down, and they were now wandering through town and being friendly with the tourists. In exchange, they were getting plenty of pets.

"They sure are loving the attention." Violet giggled.

"I wonder where Fred is," Jessie said. They looked but couldn't see the author anywhere. "It seems like this is just the sort of thing he'd like to see for his book. Horses running wild through town is pretty exciting."

Jessie and Violet were able to round up a few horses right on Main Street. All the horses they approached were gentle. They collected two horses and were about to return to the stable with them when one of the riders from the Pony Express demonstration walked over.

"I can take those two back to the stable so you can keep tracking down the horses," he said. "Thanks to you, Henry, and Benny, we've tracked down all of them. But I can't find Sofia. Could you help us one last time and find her, to let her know we've rounded up all the horses?"

"Count on us!" Violet said. "Jessie, let's check down by the train platform. I saw hoofprints leading that way."

Jessie tapped the reins, and they rode off toward the platform. There was one set of prints in the dirt road, some so clear and fresh that Violet could make out the curved shape of the horse's shoe.

"Look, there's a horse up by the train," Jessie said.

When they got closer, Violet pointed. Sofia's horse was tied to a hitching post near the back of the train. They could tell it was Sofia's because it was wearing the mochila.

"What's it doing out here by the train?" Violet asked. "And where's Sofia?"

The door to the rear car opened and out hopped Sofia onto the horse's saddle before plopping down. Jessie was impressed how easily Sofia got on and off her horse. When Sofia saw Jessie and Violet, she looked surprised. Then she smiled.

"No horses out here," she said.

"What were you doing in the train?" Violet asked.

Sofia glanced back at the train. "I came to the

station to ask the crew if they'd seen any horses. But when I got here, I heard a noise back by the rear car. That's where they keep the valuables in the safe, you know. I wanted to see if something fishy was going on. I thought I saw someone, but after investigating, now I'm not sure. Something still feels off."

"Was someone trying to steal from the safe?" Jessie gasped.

"If they were, letting all the horses loose would be a great distraction," Violet said. "I'm glad I kept my stone in my bag."

Sofia cleared her throat. "Anyway. Were you able to find the other horses?"

"Yes. We came to let you know that everything's taken care of," Violet said.

Sofia sighed with relief. "That's great news. Thank you so much...Now there's no worry about missing the next part of your tour. Which, if I remember correctly, will be Clear Springs Ranch, just a couple hours by train up the track."

"A ranch!" Violet exclaimed. "I can't wait."

Sofia grinned.

"It's great fun. There will be a rodeo and some cowhand demonstrations. And after all your hard work rounding up the horses today, you'll fit right in!" she said.

CONTINUE TO PAGE 75

SWEET SHOPPE

While the children were trying to decide what to do, Benny's stomach grumbled. He rubbed his belly.

"All this talk of candy is making me hungry," he said.

Henry chuckled. "All right. I guess that settles it. Sofia, good luck rounding up the horses."

Sofia tipped her hat. "Leave it to me. I'll make sure the horses get back to the stable, and clear the tracks so the train can leave on time. You all enjoy the candy shop. I promise it'll be worth it!"

Sofia clucked her tongue, and away she went on her horse. The Aldens followed Main Street back into the busier part of the town. Near the saloon, they saw a building with white-and-red-striped eaves. Big wood blocks were carved in the shapes of letters and painted bright, playful colors. The letters read: SWEET SHOPPE.

"Why does 'shop' have those extra letters?" Benny asked.

"It's an old-timey way of writing *shop*," Jessie explained. "Because it's an old-timey candy shop, I guess!"

Inside, the shop was decorated in pinks and reds and blues and smelled like sweet waffle-cone batter. A glass case ran the length of the room, full of sweets and piles of wrapped candies. One section of the case had tubs of delicious-looking ice cream. Benny leaned against the case and licked his lips.

"That ice cream looks soooo good," he said. "Can I have a scoop?"

"We had a big breakfast, so I think it should be all right," Henry said. He addressed the clerk next. "Excuse me. Could we have four ice-cream cones, please?"

"Sure you can," said the clerk. "What flavors would you like?"

"Chocolate, please!" Benny said.

"I'd also like chocolate, please," said Violet.

"I think we all want chocolate," Jessie added with a laugh.

"Well, I have some bad news and some good news," said the clerk. "The bad news is we just ran out of chocolate. But the good news is I was going to make some more right now. We make our ice cream here the old-fashioned way. If you kids are interested, we could make the ice cream together, and you can see how it was done."

Benny's and Violet's eyes lit up.

"That sounds like fun!" Benny said.

"We still have plenty of time before the train leaves for the next stop, since the Pony Express show was cut short," Jessie said. "And I've always wanted to see how ice cream was made."

The clerk looked pleased as pie. "Great! Because making ice cream is also a lot of work, and I could use the help. Meet me out front on the porch, and I'll be right there."

The porch outside the candy shop had a row of wooden chairs and was shaded from the bright sun. After a few minutes, the clerk came outside with a big wooden barrel. He set it down with a thud and opened it up. Inside was a metal cannister with a lid.

"What's that in the can?" Benny asked.

"Those are the paddles," said the clerk. "They churn the cream—here, go ahead and pour it in."

Benny and Violet took turns pouring two big jugs of cream into the metal cannister. The clerk also gave them chocolate powder to add before they sealed the cannister. Next the clerk brought out a bag of ice that they used to fill the wooden tub around the cannister. Finally, they added salt to the ice.

"Now comes the tiring part," the clerk said. He set a hand crank on top of the cannister. "The salt pulls the moisture out of the cream, and the ice makes it cold. Start cranking!"

"I didn't know making ice cream was so much work!" Benny said as he turned the handle with both hands.

"And ice was hard to come by in the Old West," added the clerk. "They didn't have freezers."

"Today, we always have ice cream in the freezer," said Jessie. "Well, *almost* always," she added, giving Benny a playful grin.

"It must have been a really special treat back then," said Violet.

The children took turns cranking the handle, which swirled the cream inside the cannister. It took about forty-five minutes before the cream started to thicken up and look like ice cream.

"We did it!" Violet said when it was finally ready. She wiped some sweat from her forehead. "What a workout."

"You kids did a great job," said the clerk. "In thanks for help, your cones are on the house!"

Benny was confused. "The cones aren't on the house," he said. "They're inside. I saw them!"

"He means they are complimentary," Henry laughed. "Free!"

The Aldens sat on the porch and enjoyed their frosty ice cream. Making it had been hard work, but ice cream had never tasted sweeter.

When their bellies were full, the four children said good-bye to the shop owner and headed toward the train to meet up with Grandfather and the rest of the tour group.

"What's going on up at the platform?" Jessie asked.

Ahead, a large group was gathered next to the train. People were whispering to one another. Everyone seemed worried. The only person who didn't seem upset was Fred, the author, who looked excited.

"This is it," he said to one of the others. "This is the kind of drama I've been waiting for! A real robbery!"

"Robbery?" Henry gasped.

The crowd hushed as Mr. Kinsey walked onto the platform and cleared his throat.

"Hello, everyone," he began. "I have some distressing news. While we were touring Regions Station, someone entered the rear car of the train and broke into the safe. Everything inside was stolen. If you had belongings stored in the safe, please come and see me. Everyone else, please prepare to board. We will be skipping the rest of the tour and heading straight to the final destination, where we can alert the authorities."

"Oh no!" Violet gasped.

"Why would someone break into that safe?" Henry asked out loud. "The only thing in there were the stones people found from Nugget Mine."

"And Grandfather's slippers," Benny added.

The only person who didn't seem upset was Fred. In fact, he seemed giddy, with a twinkle in his eye.

"I wonder how the thief got away with it!" he said.

"Well, one thing's for sure," Violet said. "Our adventure on the Wild West Express is over."

THE END

TO FOLLOW A DIFFERENT PATH, GO, TO PAGE 59.

RANCH 'N' RODEO

As the Aldens arrived to board the train to the next stop, they ran into Sofia on the platform.

"Thanks for all your help today," she said. "If we're lucky, we'll meet again!"

"Are you coming on the train?" Benny asked.

"No, sir. But the other riders and I like to ride along the tour trail sometimes, just for a taste of what real Pony Express riders might have experienced. If you see us, give us a holler."

Then Sofia tipped her hat and leaped from the station platform down onto her horse, where it was waiting on the street.

"We should keep an eye out for suspicious people," Jessie said. She lowered her voice. "Violet and I think there may be a real bandit on board the train. I saw someone get on back in Nugget Mine, and when we were helping Sofia with the horses, she said she saw someone snooping around the car where the safe is."

"A real bandit?" yelled Benny. Jessie shushed him.

"Do you know who it might be?" said Henry.

"Not yet," said Violet. "But we didn't see Fred anywhere when we were returning the horses."

"That guy seems to want to make things interesting," Benny said.

"Anyway, just stay alert," Jessie said. "Whether it's jewels or just to make things dramatic, we don't know what the person is really after."

Before long, the train departed. Right on time, thanks to Mr. Kinsey. The Aldens had lunch with Grandfather in the dining car, and they shared stories about their morning activities. After a few short hours, the train horn blew, and they heard the whistling of the wheels as they came into the station of another small town. It was just one main street with a few shops, like Regions Station. The biggest difference was that Clear Springs had a small hotel, right across the street from the train platform.

"All passengers, this is the engineer speaking. Clear Springs is an overnight stop," Mr. Kinsey said over the loudspeaker. "All tour passengers are welcome to spend the night in town or on the train. There is also a camping excursion available. Please speak with the attendants to arrange your stay. Train leaves at exactly 8:20 a.m. tomorrow morning. We will not be late."

"He sounds cheerful as usual," Grandfather joked.

The Aldens left the train. Alex was waiting on the platform holding a sign that read *Ranch Tour.* Violet tugged on Henry's sleeve.

"That must be where we go to visit the Clear Springs Ranch," she said.

"I want to go," Benny added. "It sounds like fun, and I like Alex's tours."

"Then you four should definitely visit the ranch," Grandfather said. "My backside is sore from the train, so I'm going to go for a walk through town. I should call home and see how Mrs. McGregor is doing. I'll meet you all back here after your tour, and we'll decide where we want to spend the night."

Fred, the author, was first in line for the ranch tour. He was wearing his cowboy hat and was practically shaking with excitement.

"When I was a boy, I always dreamed of being a cowboy," he was telling Alex. "Getting that gold buckle—oh, the glory! Unfortunately, I was never able to compete."

"That's a shame," Alex said with a friendly smile. "At least today you'll be able to see some action. I believe some of the kids in town are doing practice today for breakaway roping."

"What's breakaway roping?" Henry asked.

"And what's a gold buckle?" Benny added.

"Breakaway is a rodeo event where a cowboy uses their lasso to catch a calf as it tries to run away," Alex explained.

"And a gold buckle is what you get if you win in a tournament and become the champion!" added Fred.

"But we'll learn more about all of that at the ranch," Alex said. She waved the other members of the tour group over as a shuttle van pulled up next to the platform. A minute later, they were off.

It was barely ten minutes before the van turned onto the gravel driveway of Clear Springs Ranch. Benny pointed at the rows of covered wagons sitting out on the big front lawn.

"What are those?" he asked.

"Conestoga wagons," Alex said. "They're the kind some of the settlers used when they migrated west. Billy, the owner of the ranch, can tell you more about them later if you ask."

The van parked near the main ranch building. The children could hear the bellowing of steer coming from the barn at the back of the ranch. A man wearing blue jeans, chaps, and a suede jacket came out to meet them. He also wore a wide-brimmed cowboy hat.

"His hat's even bigger than yours," Benny said.

"Then I will need to get a bigger one," Fred replied.

"Howdy, folks!" called the cowboy. "My name's Billy. I'm the owner of Clear Springs Ranch. I also lead the wagon camping tour. You probably saw the wagons on your way up. Y'all want to see some of what we do out here on the ranch? Well, come on back to the arena!"

Everyone followed Billy. Behind the main ranch building was a large barn that opened into a covered arena. Children and adults alike were cheering and shouting for a boy about Jessie's age, who was waiting patiently on horseback. One of the adults opened the gate to a small pen beside the horse, and a brown calf dashed out. The moment the calf ran into the arena, the boy on horseback burst out in chase, swinging a lasso. He threw the lasso and the loop landed around the calf's neck. As soon as the rope encircled the calf, the boy let go of the rope and the calf slowed to a trot. The crowd cheered.

"This is breakaway roping," Billy explained as one of the adults retrieved the calf, using the lasso like a leash to lead it back to another pen. "The goal is to show how skilled you are with a lasso on horseback. It's very difficult to catch a moving target with just a rope, especially when you're in the saddle. That there's my son, Cody. I taught him everything I know."

Cody saw the tour group and waved. Billy waved back.

"I didn't know kids could be cowboys," Benny said.

"It's hard work, but out on the ranch, everyone needs to lend a helping hand," Billy replied. "Cody started roping when he was just eight years old. He helps round up the cattle every afternoon now. And he helps with the wagon camping tour. Sure makes life easier on his old man."

"Does anyone want to try throwing a rope?" Alex asked.

"Me!" Benny said.

"I'd like to give it a try too," said Jessie. She was inspired by seeing Cody's skill in the ring.

Alex brought them out to the yard in front of the barn, where they could still see inside the arena if they wanted to watch more breakaway roping. In the yard, there was a wooden sawhorse that was about the same size as a calf. Alex handed Jessie a rope lasso. It was lightweight and a little rough on her hands.

"Here. Now, you hold it like this," Alex said.

Alex showed Jessie how to hold the rope. She held the coil of slack in one hand and held the loop in the other. With a little bit of practice, Jessie learned how to swing the loop over her head.

"When you're ready, give it a throw toward the head," Alex said. "Just like you're throwing a baseball!"

Jessie gave it toss. The loop flew out and bounced off the back of the sawhorse. Benny and some of the other people from the tour gave a cheer.

"Next time!" Benny said. "I bet you can do it, Jessie!"

Jessie blushed. She wound up the rope and got ready to try again. On the second time, the loop went right around the sawhorse's head. Benny clapped and clapped for her.

"Wow, Jessie! You're a natural," Alex said with a wink.

Everyone had a chance to try. Even Benny was able to catch the sawhorse with some encouragement from Jessie and Alex.

The only person who couldn't get the loop around the sawhorse's head was Fred. After two tries, and two misses, he got frustrated.

"This is silly," he said with a huff. "It doesn't matter. This isn't even the real thing. I want to rope real cattle!" With an even bigger huff, he tossed his lasso away and stomped back into the arena.

"I'll bet if he tried a little longer, he would be able to get it," Benny said.

"He seems like an impatient guy," Alex said. "Unfortunately, most of the work done in the Old West took time and patience. Running a ranch was an important part of settlement life. People would spend their whole lives perfecting skills like horseback riding, steering cattle, and farming."

After a long day at the ranch, the tour group gathered on the front lawn with Billy and Cody. They were bringing cattle out and hooking their harnesses up to the wagons.

"Hope y'all had a good time at the ranch," Billy said when he saw they were heading out. "And I'll see some of you tonight on the camping tour!"

They said good-bye to Billy and climbed into the shuttle van to head back to Clear Springs. The sky was pink and beginning to get dark.

Jessie rubbed her sore arms as the van pulled onto the road.

"What do you think, Benny? Ready to become a cowboy?" she asked.

"I don't know. It's a lot of work," Benny said. "And I'm hungry!"

"Luckily, dinner's up next," Henry said. "I just got a text from Grandfather. He wants to know whether we want to go on the wagon camping trip or spend the night on the train in the sleeping car."

"How often do we get the chance to camp outside?" Jessie asked. "Remember when we used to sit around the fire, back when we lived in the boxcar?"

"Then again, there might be a bandit afoot," Henry reminded everyone. "If there's someone interested in the safe, we might find out more if we stay on the train."

"Look!" Benny said, pointing out the window.

Everyone looked. A group of horse riders in costumes galloped alongside the road. The horses' coats were shining with sweat, their manes and tales rippling in the wind. Violet gasped when she recognized the rider with the braid.

"That's Sofia and the others from the stable in Regions Station!" she said. "Looks like they decided to come out on the adventure after all!"

The Aldens waved as the van came alongside the riders. Sofia took off her hat and waved it in the air, a big grin across her face.

Back in town, Grandfather was waiting for them at the tour van stop. "Did you have fun out at the ranch?" he asked.

"Yes! Jessie and I are going to become cowboys," Benny said.

"I'm not sure about that," Jessie laughed.

"Well, I hope you worked up an appetite," said Grandfather. "Did you decide where you wanted to spend the night?"

IF THE CHILDREN SLEEP UNDER THE STARS,
GO TO PAGE 86.

IF THE ALDENS SPEND THE NIGHT ON THE TRAIN,
GO TO PAGE 96.

UNDER THE STARS

"We've already spent a few nights on the train," Henry said, tapping his chin. "Maybe it would be fun to have a change of scenery."

"Not only that, but how often do you get to camp under the stars in the desert?" Jessie added.

"It's turning into a really lovely evening," Violet added. "The stars are out, and it's not chilly at all. It would be a good night to be outdoors."

"Let's camp!" Benny said.

Grandfather chuckled and nodded. "I think you children have made the right decision. Experiences like these don't happen every day, so you should soak it up while you can," he said. "I, on the other hand, think I will stay at the hotel in town. My back has been complaining a bit, so I could use a sleep in a full-size bed."

The Aldens said good night to Grandfather and met Alex on the platform, where she gathered the people from the group who wanted to go on the wagon camping trip. Fred was waiting with the group. As always, he looked very excited.

"When will the wagons arrive?" he asked Alex.

"The steer travel much slower than the tour van, but they should still be here soon," Alex said. "The campsite is a short ways from here, on the other side of the train tracks. If we're all ready to go, we can walk over."

Alex led the way down the platform stairs. The group walked out into the wide desert that stretched on the other side of the tracks. Benny looked back as they followed a thin trail away from town.

"It does get very dark out here at night," Alex said over her shoulder. They reached a clearing in the sagebrush at the end of the gravel trail. Alex pointed. "And here come the wagons, right on time!"

Lit by the gentle gold of the setting sun, the silhouettes of six covered wagons were heading toward them. Each covered wagon was drawn by two steer. The ground rumbled under the heavy hooves and wheels of the wagons. Billy was sitting at the front of the lead wagon, and he waved his hat as they pulled up. His son Cody was driving another nearby.

"Whoa, whoa!" he called, tugging on the reins. The steer slowed, and all six wagons came to a halt. Billy hopped down. "Howdy, everybody! Great to see you again. Are y'all ready for some real outdoor campin'?"

"Am I ever!" Benny said.

Billy started the camping trip by forming six groups. Each group was assigned a campsite leader. The Aldens and Fred were the only ones from the Wild West Express train tour, so they were grouped together. Their campsite leader was Cody. He opened the canvas flap at the rear of the wagon.

"Go ahead and take a look," he said. "You can also put your backpacks and belongings in here for safekeeping overnight. We'll be sleeping out under the stars."

The Aldens explored the wagon while Cody started a fire. The wagon had a bottom carriage built from wood, with a curved bottom. The top part was made of canvas stretched over wooden support beams, sort of like a tent. It also had four huge wheels, each of them taller than Benny.

The sound of horse's hooves interrupted them. A group of horse riders rode up to the wagon campsite. Sofia gave them all a big grin when they saw her.

"Hey, y'all," she said. "Fancy seeing you here!"

"Hey, Sofia," Cody said. "You just ride in from Regions Station?"

"Yup. The tour comin' through the past few days gave me the adventure itch, so we decided to make the ride out to Carson City. We thought we'd settle down here in Clear Springs for the night. But it's such a nice night out, and we saw y'all had your fires started. Thought we might camp out for a change instead of staying in town. Mind if we join you?"

Cody tipped his hat. "Sure thing, Sofia. You can tie your horses to the back of the wagon."

"Thank you kindly, Cody," Sofia said. Next, she turned to the Aldens. "You children enjoying your time? Find any more fancy stones?" she asked, looking at Violet.

Violet blushed, but Benny spoke up. "We haven't found any more treasure, but me and Jessie are going to be real live cowboys."

"Is that so?" Sofia said warmly. "Well then, sleeping under the stars suits you. Hope y'all have a nice night!"

The group warmed their hands by the fire while Cody got supper started. The sky had become a deep, dark blue, and the air was a little cool. But right by the fire, it was nice and warm, and around them, they could see the fires from the other wagon groups. Sofia and the horse riders set up their own camp nearby. All in all, it was a pleasant evening. Cody even baked cornbread muffins using just the campfire.

"Cody, do you know any spooky stories?" Violet asked. It just felt right to ask, sitting around the fire while they ate.

"Oh sure, I know plenty! Out here in the west, you know, there are all manner of strange creatures," Cody said. "Let me see...Oh, I know!"

Trouble on the Wild West Express

Cody pulled his cowboy hat down low over his forehead and leaned toward the fire so the light cast dancing shadows across his face. He lowered his voice.

"Have y'all heard of the hellidad?" he asked. "One of the most peculiar creatures in these parts. My pop, Billy, told me he seen it once when he was driving cattle late one night last summer. Must've been just round this area too. In the dead of the night, see, he spotted a creature looked like a cross between a zebra and an ostrich."

"What!" Henry said with a laugh. "A zebra and an ostrich?"

"Yessir," Cody said. He looked serious. "And it come galloping along on its four striped zebra legs, big ol' tongue floppin' around outside of its ostrich mouth. But before my pop could say nothin' about it, it disappeared into the night. Now, he'd been out late driving those steer, and he was real tired. So he decided to camp out the night and finish the job in the morning. He laid his head down and got some shut-eye."

"Did the hellidad come back?" Fred, the author,

asked with a shaky voice. He had been jotting in his notebook, but when Cody started telling the spooky story, he forgot about writing his notes. Now, he gripped his notebook and his pen tightly.

"Well, the next morning, my pop woke up cuz he felt a big, wet tongue on the back of his head. But when he opened his eyes, the creature that done it run off, and he's had a bald spot on the back of his head ever since. My ma says it was one of the steer, but my pops swears it was that hellidad. That's why he wears that cowboy hat all the time!"

They shared more stories by the light of the campfire. Some of the stories were funny, but some were downright spooky. When Benny got frightened, Henry reminded him that these were just tall tales, made-up stories for fun.

When it was time for bed, the children changed into their pajamas and stowed their backpacks and belongings in the wagon. Then they pulled up their sleeping bags and fell asleep thinking of wild critters.

The next morning, Benny woke to a shaking below his pillow. At first, he thought it might be

the hellidad galloping through their campsite. But when he threw back his sleeping bag, he didn't see a striped ostrich trying to lick him bald. He saw a big plume of steam coming from the train!

"Everyone, wake up! The train's leaving without us!" Benny shouted.

"What's that?" mumbled Cody. "The train's not scheduled to leave for another two hours!"

Everyone scrambled to their feet. The train was definitely moving.

"Is Mr. Kinsey leaving without us?" Benny asked. "I didn't know he was *that* grumpy!"

"Where's Fred?" Henry asked. Fred's sleeping bag was empty. The author was nowhere to be found.

"We'll have to worry about him later," Jessie said. "What should we do?"

"We can take the wagon," Cody said.

But Violet had another idea. She pointed to the campsite where Sofia and the other riders were camping. "What about the horses?" she suggested. "Maybe we could borrow them to catch up to the train."

"Whatever we do, we have to do it fast," Henry said. "If we don't get going, the train is going to leave without us!"

IF THE ALDENS HOP ON THE CONESTOGA WAGON, GO TO PAGE 101.

IF THE CHILDREN RIDE THE PONY EXPRESS HORSES, GO TO PAGE 106.

NIGHT TRAIN

"I want to spend the night on the train," Henry said.

Violet nodded in agreement. "It's not very often we get to sleep in a place like this," she said.

"It's like when we used to live in the boxcar!" Benny added.

"Very well. Let's have supper on the train, too, then," Grandfather suggested.

The five of them had a delicious, warm meal in the cozy dining car. After dinner, they settled into their compartment aboard the train. Jessie wrote in her diary about their day while Henry took a book from his backpack and read aloud to Violet and Benny. Grandfather read a local newspaper he'd picked up in town, turning the page every so often. It was the perfect relaxing end to a busy day.

Later that night, the Aldens were awakened by a rumbling. Violet rubbed her eyes.

"Is the train moving?" she mumbled.

"No, it's not the train," Henry said, getting out of his bunk. "Let's go out and see what's going on."

Still in their pajamas, the four Aldens and Grandfather hurried out to the train platform. Other tourists wandered out, yawning and looking around. The rumbling was getting closer. They could see lights coming down the road that crossed in front of the platform, but they weren't headlights from a car. They were wagon lanterns!

"Look there," Alex said. "Everyone, stay on the platform!"

The platform shook as six Conestoga wagons, drawn by galloping cattle, rattled down the road. The cattle looked spooked, moaning and wailing in their fright. The lanterns hanging off the wagons swung back and forth. Luckily, it seemed there were no people in the wagons, and all the tourists who had slept on the train were safe on the platform. It was loud and strange, but no one was hurt.

A moment later, a few cowboys on horseback rode up. The Aldens recognized Billy and Cody.

"What just happened?" Alex asked.

"Someone spooked the cattle out at the camping tour site," Billy shouted. "Alex, can you get on a horse and help us get control of the herd? They're running right down the main street!"

"I think it's safest if we go back inside the train," Grandfather said calmly. "Alex and the others will take care of the cattle. They can be quite dangerous when they're spooked."

The children agreed and went back into the train, along with the other passengers. Benny held on to Jessie's hand.

"I hope no one at the campsite was hurt," he said.

"Me too," added Jessie.

"I wonder what scared the cattle like that," Henry said.

Violet frowned when they got back to their sleeping compartment. Her bag was open on her bed, and all of her belongings were scattered about.

"Oh no, what happened?" Grandfather asked. He looked back in the corridor, but there was no one to be seen. "Did someone break in while we were all out on the platform?"

Violet looked through her belongings to see if anything was missing. Most of her things were there, but there was one thing that wasn't. She sighed.

"Someone stole the rock I found back at Nugget Mine," she said.

"I'm sorry, Violet," Jessie said.

"It's okay," Violet replied, even though she was still disappointed. She had come to really like that rock and was eager to add it to her collection back at home.

Benny took out his pop-top and offered it to Violet. "I know it's not the same, but you can have my good luck charm if you want."

Violet gave a small smile. "Thanks, Benny."

"Do you think the thief spooked the cattle to cause a distraction?" Henry asked. "Who would do such a thing just to get at a little stone that Violet had?"

Grandfather shook his head, stroking his beard. "We may never know," he said. "The thief is long gone. I'm beginning to think that rock of yours was even more important than we thought."

THE END

TO FOLLOW A DIFFERENT PATH, GO TO PAGE 85.

ON THE WAGON

"Let's take the wagon!" Henry said, making a quick decision. "Come on, everyone!"

The Aldens climbed into the wagon, and Cody released the steer from the hitch. He leaped into the front seat and snapped the reins. With a bumpy lurch, the wagon shook into motion.

"It's not going very fast," Jessie said.

"Cattle aren't as fast as horses," Cody shouted back. "But the train will take some time to speed up. We should still be able to make it!"

Cody drove the wagon up along the tracks. The train was up ahead, picking up steam, but it still seemed like they would make it.

"Hold on to your hats!" Cody called back.

They neared the rear car of the train. Henry

pushed back the flap of the wagon. They were catching up, and it looked like they were going to make it.

CRRR-ACK!

The sound of snapping wood rang out. Splinters flew through the air. Henry yelped and fell back into the wagon as it swerved and skidded to a halt on a broken wheel. Everyone got out and watched the train as it continued on ahead, leaving them in the dust.

"Are you all right?" called a voice. It was Mr. Kinsey. He was jogging down the tracks from the platform, still in his pajamas.

"Yes, we're all fine," Jessie said. "Although the wagon has seen better days... Wait a minute, Mr. Kinsey. Why aren't you on the train?"

"We thought you left without us!" Benny said.

"I wouldn't do that," Mr. Kinsey said, crossing his arms. "I always leave on time. Not a minute too soon, not a minute too late. I was sleeping peacefully in the motel when the train started pulling away."

Everyone was quiet for a moment as they

watched the train disappear into the distance.

Jessie said, "Mr. Kinsey, I've been wondering. Now that we know you didn't have anything to do with the strange things happening on the train... You seemed grumpy back in the saloon in Regions Station. Why was that?"

Mr. Kinsey shook his head. "That? Oh, I'm sorry. The truth is, I've lived all my life in this area, and sometimes tourists get me frustrated. They don't think about the fact that people actually live here. They only want to fantasize about the olden days."

"Like Fred?" Benny said.

Mr. Kinsey nodded.

"Speaking of Fred," said Henry. "Where is he?"

"Maybe he got up early and went to the train," Jessie suggested.

"Do you think he has something to do with this?" Violet asked.

"At this rate, there's no telling," said Mr. Kinsey. "The good news is, even if the bandit got away, the train will have to stop at the next town to resupply the engine with water. The best thing we can do is head into town and try to find a ride to meet up."

The Aldens nodded to one another, and Benny let out a big sigh. It was a shame their tour had ended on this note, but there wasn't much they could do about it now.

THE END

TO FOLLOW A DIFFERENT PATH, GO TO PAGE 95.

RIDING THE PONIES

"The horses will be much faster than the wagon," Cody said. "Good luck!"

The Aldens grabbed their backpacks and dashed to the campsite where Sofia was staying with the other horse riders. Her friends were waking up, rubbing their eyes. But Sofia was nowhere to be found.

"Can we borrow your horses?" Henry asked. "Our train is leaving without us!"

"Be careful!" said one of the riders.

Henry and Jessie each hopped aboard a horse, taking Benny and Violet with them. The horses were well trained and responded right away. Within moments, they were galloping after the train.

"The train will take some time to speed up. We

might be able to make it," Henry said.

"Who's that up ahead?" Jessie shouted, pointing to the tracks near the platform. Someone was running behind the train, waving his arms. As they got closer, they saw that it was Mr. Kinsey, the engineer.

"Wait, wait!" he yelled after the train. He saw the Aldens coming. "Get aboard and tell whoever is driving the train to stop!" he cried.

Henry saluted. He held tight to the reins. Although the train was going too fast for Mr. Kinsey, it wasn't too fast for the horses yet. They easily caught up to the rear car, but the train was slowly picking up speed. If they didn't get on quickly, the train would get away.

"Get ready, Benny," he said. "See that ladder? Grab on and open the door. I'll be right behind you!"

There was a ladder bolted to the outside of one of the middle cars. Henry's horse galloped up alongside it, and Benny reached out. He grasped the ladder and climbed on. Henry kicked off the stirrups and grabbed the ladder too. The horse galloped away from the train and back to its riders.

Benny opened the train hatch, and he and Henry climbed inside. A moment later, Violet and Jessie followed. They all huffed and panted from the excitement. They had made it!

"Now, what in the world is going on?" said Jessie. "I thought maybe we were just late, but Mr. Kinsey wasn't even on the train!"

"And if he's not driving, who is?" Violet asked.

"Fred wasn't at our campsite when we woke up," Benny said. "Maybe he's driving the train."

Henry thought about this. "Fred has been looking for excitement this whole trip," he said. "But I didn't think he would do something like this!"

"Sofia wasn't at her camp this morning either," Violet said. "Do you think she could be behind it?"

Jessie thought back. "Sofia also said she saw someone trying to break into the safe back in Regions Station. Maybe whoever it was decided it would be easier to steal the whole train."

Benny wrung his hands. "I don't know what to think!"

"The good news is, we're on the train now," Henry said. He looked confident and eager. "I think we should go to the front of the train and find out who's driving."

"I think we should go check the safe. We might catch the bandit red-handed!"

Benny nodded. "Time to get to the bottom of this!" he said.

IF THE ALDENS GO TO THE LOCOMOTIVE AT THE FRONT OF THE TRAIN, GO TO PAGE 110.

IF THEY GO TO THE VAULT AT THE BACK OF THE TRAIN, GO TO PAGE 118.

THE LOCOMOTIVE

"The most important thing is to find out who's driving and get them to stop the train," Henry said.

The Aldens hurried toward the front of the train, passing through car after empty car. When they were almost to the front, they were surprised to see a familiar face.

"Alex!" Benny said. "Are you the one who started the train?"

Alex the tour guide was standing near the closed door at the front of the car.

"Goodness," Alex said. "You startled me. No, I'm not the one who started the train. I got on board early to tidy up and get ready for our departure. But then the train just started moving! I came up here to see what was going on, but this door is locked from the other side. I can't make it into the locomotive to see who's driving this thing."

"It's not Mr. Kinsey, that's for sure," Benny said.

"We saw him a minute ago, before we got on the train," Violet explained.

"Then whoever is in there does not have the authority to be driving," Alex said. "We have to figure out a way to get into the locomotive and stop them."

"Is there any other way in?" Jessie asked.

Alex crossed her arms and tapped her foot in thought. "It's risky," she said to herself.

"What is?" said Benny. "Is there a secret way?"

"If someone were to climb outside of the train," said Alex, "they could enter the locomotive from the platform door. But the train is picking up speed. It could be dangerous."

"I'll do it," Henry said, rolling up his sleeves. "I've been working on my rock climbing, so I've got a lot of practice."

Alex looked unsure. But she opened the outside door. The wind rushed in, and the five of them took a look at the landscape that raced by. The train's wheels clanked and clattered on the tracks.

"Please be careful," Jessie said.

"I will," Henry replied. Then he grabbed a rung of the ladder on the outside of the train and climbed up.

The train was led by an old steam locomotive, so it wasn't going as fast as some trains. But if he fell, he would definitely get some bruises.

Henry held tight to the ladder and climbed up. There was plenty of room to stand on the roof of the train, though he crouched to keep his balance as it jostled from side to side. Henry carefully made his way to the place where the two cars were connected.

This was the riskiest part. There was a three-foot gap between the cars. He would have to jump.

"Here goes nothing!" Henry said, and he leaped as far as he could.

The train bumped as he landed on the other side. He nearly lost his footing, but he caught hold of the handrail of the ladder.

His heart was pounding. He had made it!

Henry climbed down the ladder and pulled open

the door. He slipped inside the car and approached the connecting door. He could see Jessie and Alex peering through the window and gave them a thumbs-up. Then he found the latch and turned it, unlocking the door.

A moment later, the others joined him.

"What a ride!" he said.

"I'm just glad you're all right," Jessie said. "Come on. Let's go see who's driving the train."

At the very front of the locomotive was the door to the driver's compartment. Inside was the control room, where the engineer drove the train. Alex didn't waste any time. She grabbed the handle and pulled it open.

"You!" she gasped when she saw who was inside.

It was Sofia. Beside her was a large bag filled with rocks.

Sofia spun around with a look of surprise. Then she let out a big sigh. She knew she'd been caught red-handed. Sofia picked up her bag and left the compartment when Alex gave her a stern look.

"You all keep an eye on her," Alex said. "I've got to stop the train."

Alex pulled the engine compartment door shut. The Aldens were left with Sofia, who heaved her bag onto the floor, defeated.

"So it was you who snuck onto the train back at the station in Nugget Mine," Jessie said.

Violet's eyes widened as she thought of all the strange things that had been happening during their trip. "And you must have been the one who let the horses loose in Regions Station too. There was no other bandit snooping around the train—it was you the whole time! Why?"

"I might as well tell you, now that there's no gettin' out of it," Sofia said. "Listen, I live in Nugget Mine, and my whole family lives in this area. I was on the train platform and overheard you talking to Mr. Kinsey about the fire opal. I started to worry that you might try to submit a claim. Do you know what would happen if you did that?"

Violet bent down and picked up the fire opal from Sofia's bag. It glittered amber and crimson, like a beautiful sunset. She thought about what it would take to find more of those stones, if someone really wanted to strike it rich.

"If someone submitted a mining claim, this whole area could get dug up," Violet said. "It would be bad for the people who live here."

"Exactly. I couldn't let that happen. So I borrowed one of the bandit performer's horses and hitched a ride. I figured if I took all the rocks and stones, including yours, then no one would have any proof. No one could submit a mining claim, and everyone who lives near Nugget Mine could go on with their lives."

Violet understood.

"I'm sorry, Sofia," she said. "I never planned to put in a claim. I'm not interested in getting rich on gold, and it would be especially wrong to cause all those problems just because I found this rock on a tour."

Sofia perked up, a hopeful look in her eye. "You're not going to put in a claim?" she asked.

Violet shook her head. She gave the stone to Sofia. "No," she said confidently. "Just because I found this stone doesn't mean it, or any of the land around here, is mine for the taking. I want you to have it."

Sofia smiled. She looked so happy she might cry.

"Thank you, Violet," she said. "But I want you to keep it. I did some things I ain't proud of these last couple days too. And I've got to take responsibility for that. In the end, it's not my stone either."

A loud screeching came from the rails, and the train lurched and slowed. When it had come to a stop, Alex emerged from the engine room. She dusted her hands off.

"We're not too far from the station. It should be easy enough for the rest of the tour group to catch up," she said. "I'm going to go make sure everything else is in order. Did you all get things sorted out here with Sofia?"

"Yes, I think so," Violet said.

CONTINUE TO PAGE 124

THE VAULT

"Let's check on the safe, to see if it's been tampered with," Jessie said. "If someone decided to leave with the train so they could steal out of the vault, they'll probably be heading there soon, now that the train is moving."

The children turned toward the back of the train and headed for the door that connected their car with the next. As they did, Violet saw a figure duck out of sight. Someone had been watching them through the window in the connecting door. Henry saw it too.

"Let's go!" he said.

The Aldens chased the figure through the connecting door and into the next train car. Just as they arrived, they saw someone's backside disappear through the door on the far end.

"I recognize that hat," said Benny. "That was Fred!"

"He's running toward the back of the train," Jessie said.

They caught up with Fred in the dining car, where they were surprised to see another familiar face. Grandfather was standing in the aisle with a serious look on his face. He was talking to Fred.

"You caught him, Grandfather!" Benny said. "You caught the bandit!"

When Grandfather saw his four grandchildren, his face lit up with surprise.

"Caught whom?" Grandfather asked. "Bandit? Fred was just telling me that you all had made it safely onto the train! I got up early this morning and came to the train to have my coffee and read the newspaper. To my surprise, the train took off early without everyone, including the four of you. I was so worried!"

"You mean you weren't running to the vault?" Violet asked Fred.

"What? No!" Fred said, his nose turning red with

embarrassment. "I'm afraid we already looked there. Someone opened and emptied the vault. There's nothing inside. I can only think that the thief is the one driving the train."

"If you're not the thief, then why were you on the train?" Henry continued. "Grandfather always drinks coffee and reads the newspaper early in the morning. But you left the campsite in the middle of the night. What were you up to?"

Fred coughed into his hand nervously.

"Well...you see, the truth is..." he mumbled.

"Oh, come now, Fred," Grandfather said. "Spit it out."

"Hellidads!" Fred blurted. "I couldn't stop thinking about that terrible critter from Cody's story. I quite like my hair just the way it is. So I got up and came to sleep on the train. I found your grandfather here in the dining car. I was headed up to the front of the train when I saw the four of you. Then I ran back to tell your grandfather that you were safe."

"We thought maybe you had started the train!" said Violet. "You kept saying you wanted something exciting to happen."

Fred shook his head. "No, no. To be honest, after all of this, I think I'm quite content for my life to be the way it is. I'll save my excitement for my writing from now on."

The six of them jumped when a heavy *clunk* came from ahead of them on the train. The Aldens went to the front of the car to see what had caused the noise, but when they looked out, there were no more cars!

"Oh no," Jessie gasped.

Someone had disconnected their car from the front of the train. The locomotive was speeding ahead while the dining car was slowing down. Soon they would come to a stop, while the bandit in the locomotive raced away down the tracks.

"At least Violet and I still have our lucky charms," Benny said, taking out his pop-top. Violet nodded and looked in her bag for her fire opal. But when she checked where it had been, the pocket was empty.

"Someone must have taken it from the wagon while we were sleeping," she said. "But why?"

"I'm sorry, children," Grandfather said. "But I'm glad the four of you are safe and here with me."

It was true, and the children were grateful for it. Still, they would never know who was responsible for the train robbery. The thief had gotten away.

THE END

TO FOLLOW A DIFFERENT PATH, GO TO PAGE 109.

SETTLED CLAIM

With the help of the horse riders, Billy and Cody's Conestoga wagons, and the tour shuttle van, all the people from the tour were able to catch up to the train. The Aldens were glad to be reunited with Grandfather. They were even happy to see Mr. Kinsey and Fred.

"What excitement!" Fred exclaimed when he heard about what had happened. He took out his notebook and began writing down notes. "A runaway train. Daring characters willing to brave danger to do the right thing. All I need now is a lesson for everyone to learn at the end!"

"I'm sure you'll think of one," Violet said.

"Thank you for sharing everything that happened," Fred said. "Now, I've got to go and write all this down before I forget. It's time for me to write the great American novel." And he hurried away.

They watched him go. Grandfather chuckled. "We'll reach the end of the line in a few hours. What would you children like to do in the meantime?" he asked.

The Aldens exchanged glances. They had already done so much on their Wild West trip: explored an old mine, spent the night under the stars, and even caught up to a moving train on horseback! It was hard to think of anything else.

"I just thought of a lesson to the story," Violet said.

"What's that, Violet?" Jessie asked.

"Just because you found something doesn't mean it's yours," Violet answered.

"That's a good one," Henry replied.

"I hope it's okay that I kept the pop-top I found," Benny said.

Jessie smiled. "I think that will be okay."

Benny perked up. "Hey, I just thought of what our next adventure should be!" he said.

"What's that?" asked Jessie.

"I'll give you one hint," said Benny. "It involves finding something that we missed this morning."

Benny put his hand on his tummy. It rumbled.

The children laughed. "Benny, I think you gave us two hints," said Henry.

"Finding breakfast is one adventure I am happy to join you children on," said Grandfather.

And with the train moving swiftly beneath their feet, the five of them went to do just that.

THE END

TO FOLLOW ANOTHER PATH, GO TO PAGE 118.

Check out the other Boxcar Children Interactive Mysteries!

Have you ever wanted to help the Aldens crack a case? Now you can with these interactive, choose-your-own-path-style mysteries!

978-0-8075-2850-1 · US $6.99

978-0-8075-2860-0 · US $6.99

JOURNEY ON A RUNAWAY TRAIN

Created by Gertrude Chandler Warner

HC 978-0-8075-0695-0
PB 978-0-8075-0696-7

THE CLUE IN THE PAPYRUS SCROLL

Created by Gertrude Chandler Warner

HC 978-0-8075-0698-1
PB 978-0-8075-0699-8

THE DETOUR OF THE ELEPHANTS

Created by Gertrude Chandler Warner

HC 978-0-8075-0684-4
PB 978-0-8075-0685-1

THE SHACKLETON SABOTAGE

Created by Gertrude Chandler Warner

HC 978-0-8075-0687-5
PB 978-0-8075-0688-2

THE KHIPU AND THE FINAL KEY

Created by Gertrude Chandler Warner

HC 978-0-8075-0681-3
PB 978-0-8075-0682-0

THE COMPLETE FIVE-BOOK MINISERIES

Created by Gertrude Chandler Warner

Also available as a boxed set!
978-0-8075-0693-6 · $34.95

Hardcover US $12.99 · Paperback US $6.99

Don't miss the next two books in the classic Boxcar Children series!

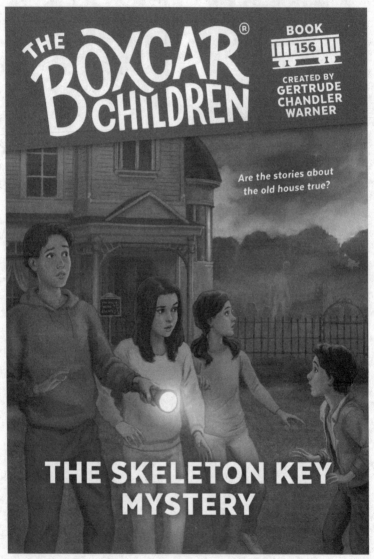

THE BOXCAR CHILDREN®

BOOK 157

CREATED BY
GERTRUDE
CHANDLER
WARNER

A science experiment turns into a big mystery!

SCIENCE FAIR SABOTAGE

HC 978-0-8075-0792-6 · US $12.99
PB 978-0-8075-0798-8 · US $6.99

Add to Your
Boxcar Children Collection
with New Books and Sets!

The first sixteen books are now available in
four individual boxed sets!

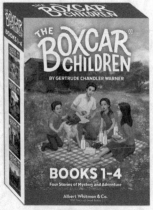

978-0-8075-0854-1 · US $24.99

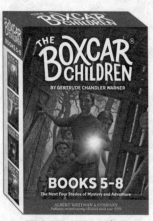

978-0-8075-0857-2 · US $24.99

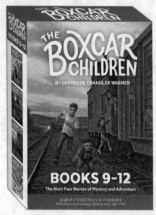

978-0-8075-0840-4 · US $24.99

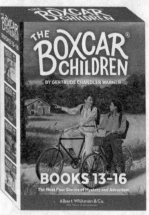

978-0-8075-0834-3 · US $24.99

The Boxcar Children 20-Book Set includes Gertrude
Chandler Warner's original nineteen books,
plus an all-new activity book, stickers,
and a magnifying glass!

978-0-8075-0847-3 · US $132.81

Look for the animated movie, *Surprise Island*!

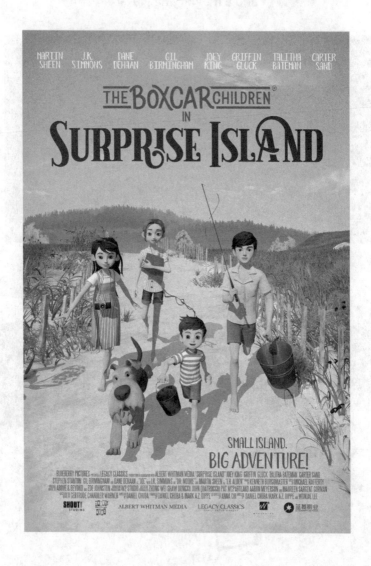

NEW!
The Boxcar Children
DVD and Book Set!

This set includes Gertrude Chandler Warner's classic chapter book in paperback as well as the animated movie adaptation featuring Martin Sheen, J.K. Simmons, Joey King, Jadon Sand, Mackenzie Foy, and Zachary Gordon.

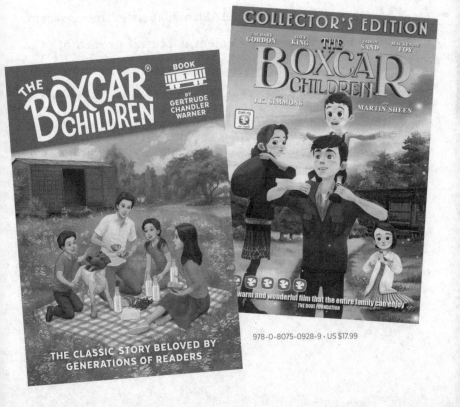

978-0-8075-0928-9 · US $17.99

GERTRUDE CHANDLER WARNER discovered when she was teaching that many readers who like an exciting story could find no books that were both easy and fun to read. She decided to try to meet this need, and her first book, *The Boxcar Children*, quickly proved she had succeeded.

Miss Warner drew on her own experiences to write the mystery. As a child she spent hours watching trains go by on the tracks opposite her family home. She often dreamed about what it would be like to set up housekeeping in a caboose or freight car—the situation the Alden children find themselves in.

While the mystery element is central to each of Miss Warner's books, she never thought of them as strictly juvenile mysteries. She liked to stress the Aldens' independence and resourcefulness and their solid New England devotion to using up and making do. The Aldens go about most of their adventures with as little adult supervision as possible— something else that delights young readers.

Miss Warner lived in Putnam, Connecticut, until her death in 1979. During her lifetime, she received hundreds of letters from girls and boys telling her how much they liked her books.